The Magic Tree

A children's story

This is a work of fiction. Names, characters, places, and incidents either are the product of the author's imagination or are used fictitiously. Any resemblance to actual persons, living or dead, events, or locales is entirely coincidental.

First edition February 2022

Book design by Andrea Ong

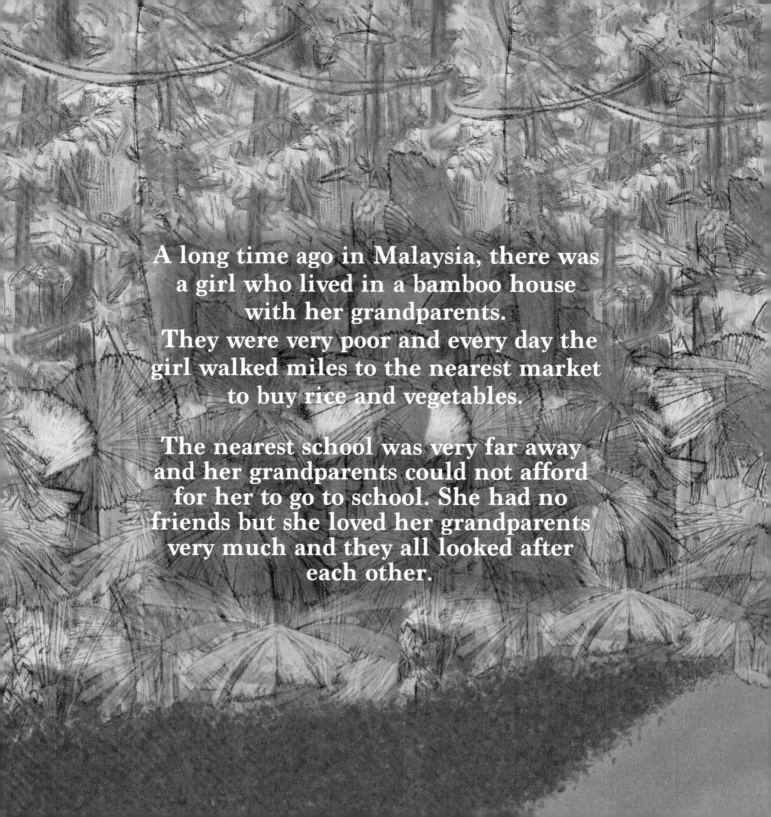

A long time ago in Malaysia, there was
a girl who lived in a bamboo house
with her grandparents.
They were very poor and every day the
girl walked miles to the nearest market
to buy rice and vegetables.

The nearest school was very far away
and her grandparents could not afford
for her to go to school. She had no
friends but she loved her grandparents
very much and they all looked after
each other.

She had lived near the rainforest all her life and her grandparents would often tell her stories about how different it used to be.

When they were little,
they saw animals and
plants from all colours of
the rainbow.

There were waterfalls
where they swam with
turtles, trees full of
hornbills' nests and
secret caves for exploring
bats and bears.

Every day, the girl walked through the rainforest to find mangoes and other fruits for her family.

While walking, she liked to imagine that the rainforest was the magical place her grandparents told her about.

In her dream she saw lots of animals who would talk to her and each other. The parrots would sing, the leopards would roar and the elephants would trumpet loudly. They would all play together and she was never alone.

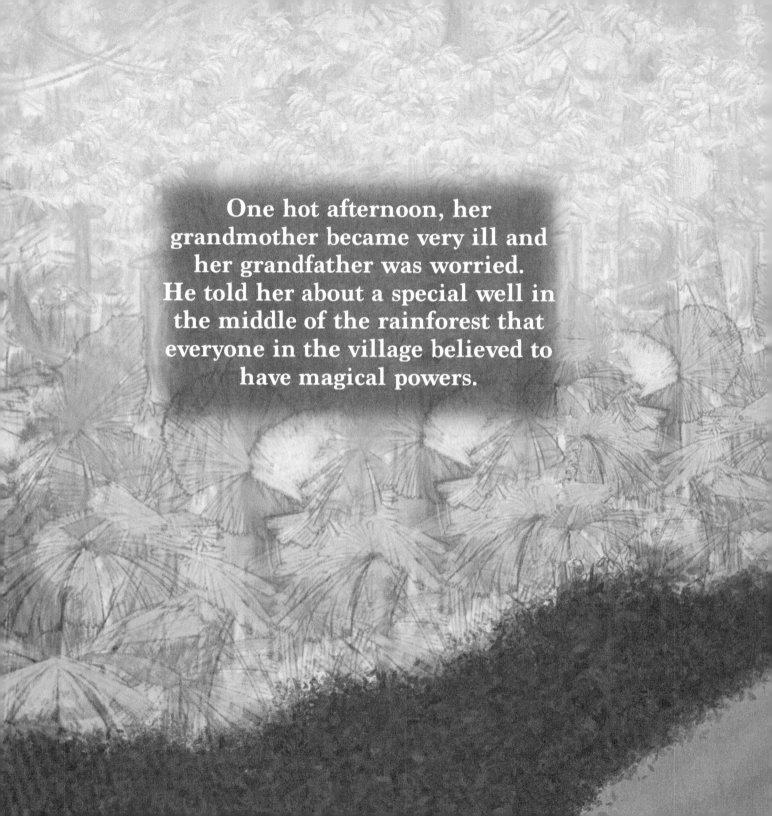

One hot afternoon, her grandmother became very ill and her grandfather was worried.
He told her about a special well in the middle of the rainforest that everyone in the village believed to have magical powers.

Immediately, she left the house with a metal bucket and nothing in front of her except the hot sun, blinding her from a distance.

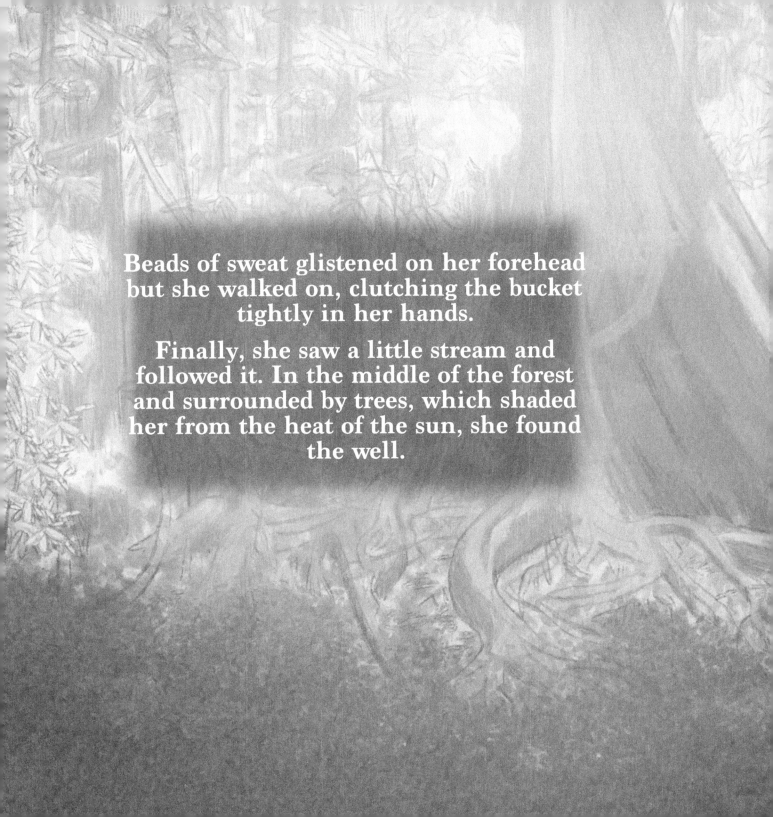

Beads of sweat glistened on her forehead but she walked on, clutching the bucket tightly in her hands.

Finally, she saw a little stream and followed it. In the middle of the forest and surrounded by trees, which shaded her from the heat of the sun, she found the well.

Where have all the animals gone? she thought to herself.
The trees were bare and there were no singing birds, hooting orangutans or croaking frogs.

She began to scoop her bucket down the well, filling it with the refreshing water.

Delighted, she looked at the water with curious eyes and then smelt it with her nose, thinking that it might be a different colour or imagined it smelt sweet like honeydew melon.

But it looked and smelled just like ordinary water.

Afterwards, she walked the long distance back.

A long time passed, she was so tired and stopped
for a few minutes to rest her shoulders and
back.

Just at that moment a strong wind blew and
dust covered her eyes. She couldn't see anything
and, in her confusion, knocked over the bucket
of water.

The girl quickly rubbed her eyes free from the dirt and saw the bucket on the floor, toppled over and empty. She began to cry, thinking of her poor grandmother who was sick and needed the magical water.

What was she going to do?
She was exhausted and knew that she had to walk back to the well, and it would be many more hours before she returned home.
By then it might be too late for her grandmother.

With determination, she picked up her bucket and turned around. Thinking of helping her grandmother gave her all the strength she needed. Finally, she arrived again at the quiet area of the forest.

Shocked, she was devastated to find that there was no more water. The glistening stream that gently flowed near the well was dry and the bottom of the well was rocks and parched earth.

The girl was inconsolable. She picked up her bucket and with a heavy heart walked away from the rainforest, towards her home.

Trudging heavily through the forest, she didn't know what she was going to tell her grandfather. They would have to take her grandmother to the village doctor, who lived miles away, and it would be very expensive. They couldn't afford it, even if they sold all their humble belongings.

The girl was deep in her own thoughts as she walked.

For a moment she looked up.

She couldn't believe her eyes but in the near distance she saw a tree that was glowing.

She rubbed her eyes
again, thinking she
was imagining it.
But she wasn't.
With growing
anticipation, she ran
faster until she
reached the tree.

It was the most magnificent thing
she had seen in her life.

The leaves were golden like the sun,
and sparkled brightly.

It was tall and resplendent, and the
rays from the sun bounced off the
leaves illuminating the whole tree.

She thought she was dreaming, but when she touched the branch, she found that it was real. The girl then reached for one of the leaves and it was smooth like a polished pearl.

She wondered if she could sell the golden leaves to pay a doctor who would make her grandmother better again.

Excitedly, she tried to take one of the leaves but it was stuck. It wouldn't come off. She pulled and tugged but nothing worked.

Then the tree spoke.
'Don't pull my leaf, you are hurting me.'

The girl was surprised and couldn't believe her ears.
'What are you?'

'I'm a magic tree.'

'If you are magic, can you help me? My grandmother
is very sick and I need to take her to a doctor.'

'Not everyone can see me. Since you found me, I will
grant you 3 wishes, over three days. Starting from
today one of my leaves will fall, and give you a wish.'

The girl was so happy that she hugged the tree
tightly.

'Ouch', said the tree.

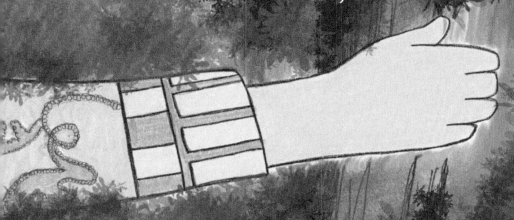

Then one leaf dropped
on the floor and the girl
took it, gripping it
tightly in her palm.

The girl ran all the way home.

When her grandfather saw his granddaughter, he was happy, but then he saw she was carrying an empty bucket.

'What shall we do?' he cried. 'Grandmother is getting worse.'

'Don't worry, Grandad. Everything will be okay.'

That night she made her
wish for the bucket to be
filled with the water from
the well.

She put the leaf in a little
wooden box her grandfather
had carved for her.

She looked up at the stars
that twinkled like fireflies
and she couldn't sleep.

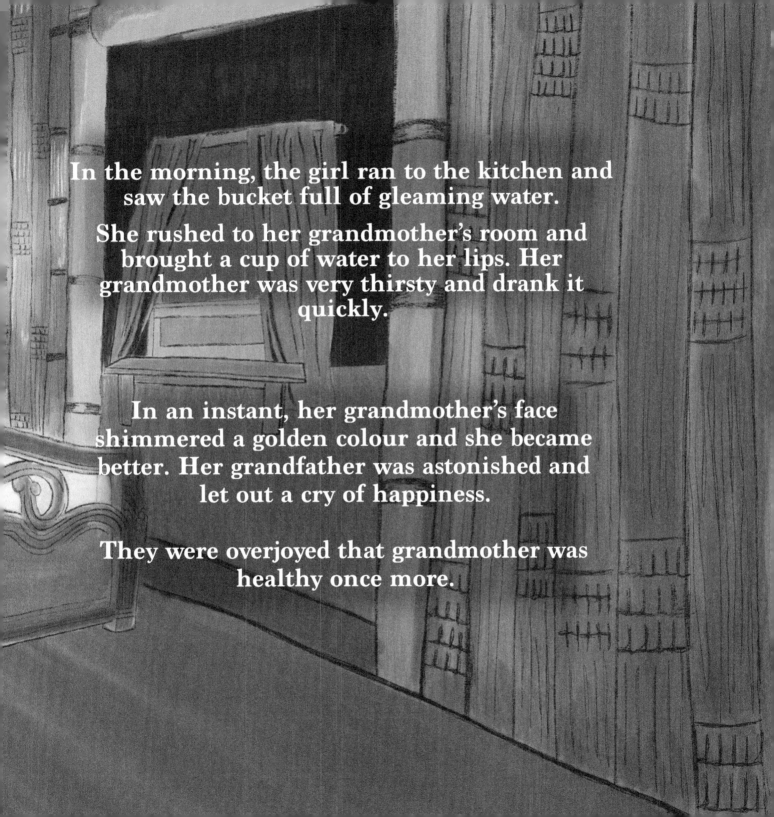

In the morning, the girl ran to the kitchen and saw the bucket full of gleaming water.

She rushed to her grandmother's room and brought a cup of water to her lips. Her grandmother was very thirsty and drank it quickly.

In an instant, her grandmother's face shimmered a golden colour and she became better. Her grandfather was astonished and let out a cry of happiness.

They were overjoyed that grandmother was healthy once more.

She was so grateful that her grandmother
was better, and she began thinking about
her next wish.

Later that day, she walked the long,
humid way to the magic tree.
As she got closer, she could see the leaves
sparkling.

Just as it promised,
another leaf had
dropped to the
floor.

She picked it up
and ran the whole
way home.

While her grandmother was cooking a delicious meal in the kitchen, the girl made her second wish and put the golden leaf in the little box.

She wished for friends. And the next day on the way to the market she met a tiger, an elephant, and an eagle. They all walked home together and she felt protected and loved.

When the sun bore too hot upon her back, the elephant opened his huge ears to shade her from the sun...

...when she became too tired, the eagle would carry her on its wings...

...and when she was so hungry that she felt she might faint, the tiger with its sharp claws, climbed the trees and collected fruit for her to eat.

After a day filled with fun, she asked her new friends to take her back to the magic tree.

Again, like the tree promised, the third leaf was waiting there.

That evening, she stayed awake all night thinking about her third and final wish.

She knew that this was her last one so she had to choose very carefully.

But she didn't know what to choose.

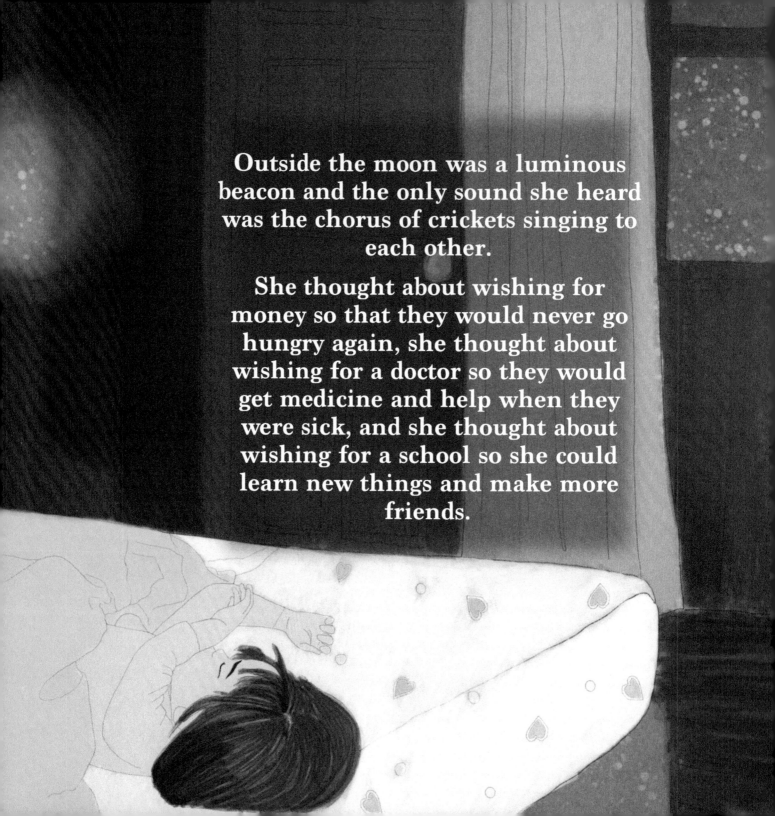

Outside the moon was a luminous beacon and the only sound she heard was the chorus of crickets singing to each other.

She thought about wishing for money so that they would never go hungry again, she thought about wishing for a doctor so they would get medicine and help when they were sick, and she thought about wishing for a school so she could learn new things and make more friends.

Finally, with the twinkling stars
falling in the sky she made her
final wish.
She carefully put the leaf inside
the box and fell asleep.

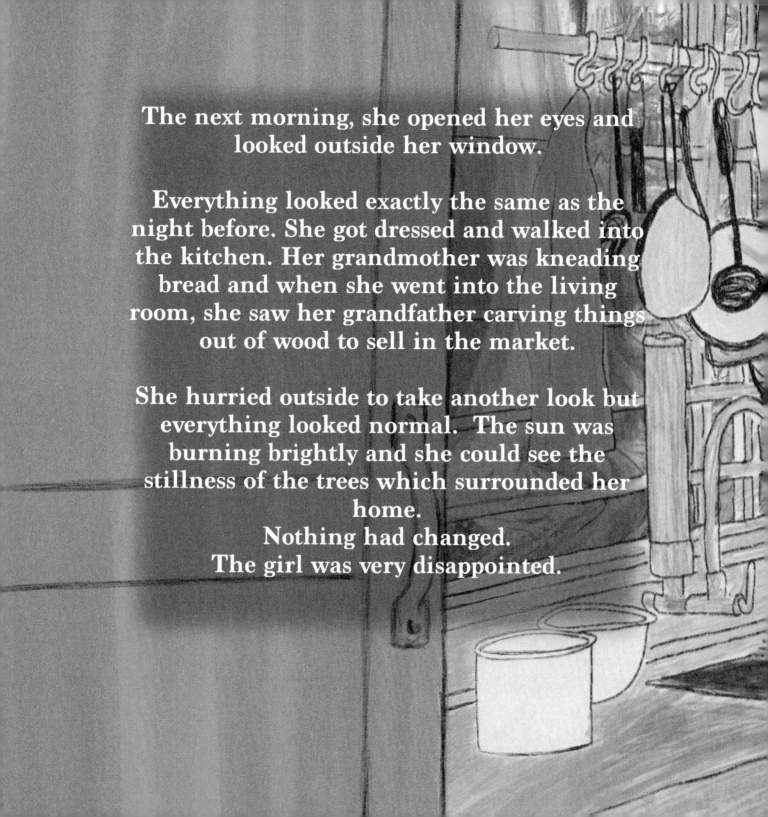

The next morning, she opened her eyes and looked outside her window.

Everything looked exactly the same as the night before. She got dressed and walked into the kitchen. Her grandmother was kneading bread and when she went into the living room, she saw her grandfather carving things out of wood to sell in the market.

She hurried outside to take another look but everything looked normal. The sun was burning brightly and she could see the stillness of the trees which surrounded her home.
Nothing had changed.
The girl was very disappointed.

She wanted to know why her wish hadn't come true. The girl put on her sandals and left the house in a hurry.

When she saw the glittering tree, she spoke to it and was upset.

'Where is my final wish? You lied to me.'
she said.

'I did not lie to you. I granted
you all of your wishes', replied
the tree.

'You only gave me two,' protested the
girl. 'When I asked for the water, you
gave it to me. Then I asked for friends
and you sent me a tiger, an elephant
and an eagle.'

'And your third and final wish?
What did you ask for next?' the tree
asked.

'I wished for the rainforest to be alive again.'

The tree repeated what he said
before. 'I granted you all three.'

'But I don't see it,' said the girl. She was
confused and getting frustrated with the
tree. 'Everything is the same. Where are
all the animals?'

'You didn't look properly. Go home, look
again and you will see.
Listen again and you will hear.'

The girl turned around and ran home.

As she came closer to her house, she was surprised to see that hours had passed and the sun was setting. She thought about what the tree said over and over again.

She noticed it was darker outside and could see faint, warm orange hues in the horizon.

While the village slept, she stayed awake and heard the night call of the owl and the chirping crickets.

She imagined all the beautiful plants and creatures, big and small that lived in the jungle and were waking up just as the moon appeared.

As she lay in bed thinking, she understood what the tree meant.

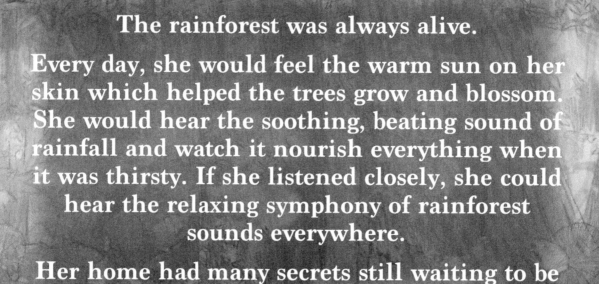

The rainforest was always alive.

Every day, she would feel the warm sun on her skin which helped the trees grow and blossom. She would hear the soothing, beating sound of rainfall and watch it nourish everything when it was thirsty. If she listened closely, she could hear the relaxing symphony of rainforest sounds everywhere.

Her home had many secrets still waiting to be discovered.

Eventually, she fell into a
deep sleep, dreaming about
everything that had happened
to her.

The next morning, she went back to the forest to say thank you to the magic tree. When she arrived, she was surprised to see that it had disappeared.

There was nothing left; not a single leaf or a trace of golden dust remained.

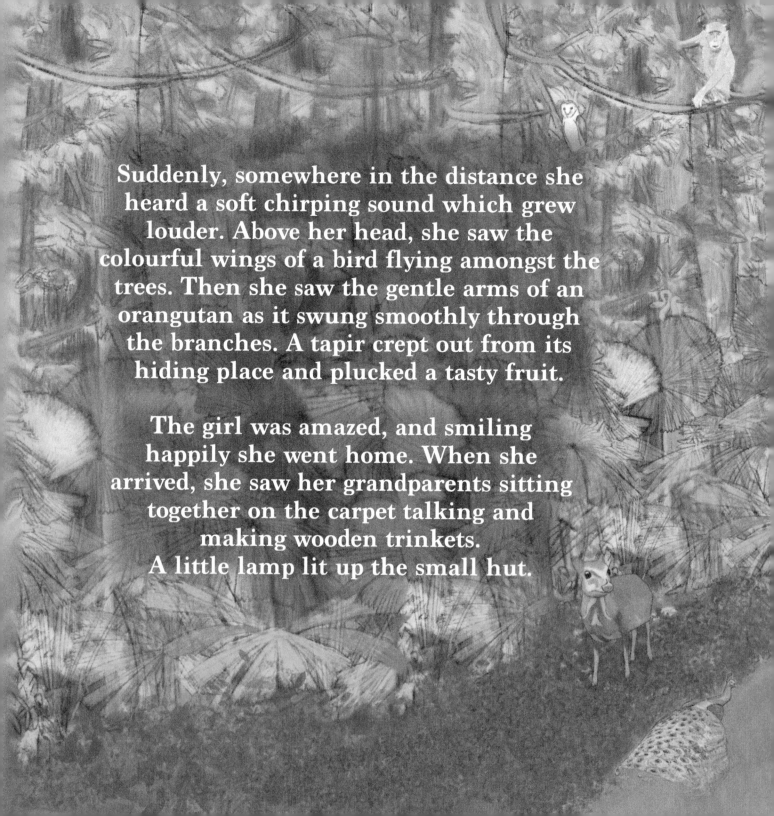

Suddenly, somewhere in the distance she heard a soft chirping sound which grew louder. Above her head, she saw the colourful wings of a bird flying amongst the trees. Then she saw the gentle arms of an orangutan as it swung smoothly through the branches. A tapir crept out from its hiding place and plucked a tasty fruit.

The girl was amazed, and smiling happily she went home. When she arrived, she saw her grandparents sitting together on the carpet talking and making wooden trinkets.
A little lamp lit up the small hut.

After dinner together, she went to her room and opened her little, wooden box.

Inside were the three golden leaves.

This story was written by Marissa Ong and illustrated by Andrea Ong.

They are sisters from the UK (born in London), with a father who is originally from Malacca, Malaysia and a mother who is originally from Dublin, Ireland. They have a big and loving family; their parents still live in the UK and there are 9 siblings in total.

At the time of writing, Marissa was teaching English to Year 2 children (6-7 years) at an International School in Kuala Lumpur. Andrea is based between London and Miami. She is also a Primary School Teacher who has taught in the UK and Japan. At the moment she creates her own teaching resources and runs her own educational website.

Marissa first wrote the story when she was about 10 years old. As a child, she loved writing ideas in a scrap book and remembers writing 'The Magic Tree' and then reading the story to her little sister, Andrea. Over the years, Marissa took the story and adapted it, while trying to keep the essence of the original story.

It wasn't until August of this 2021, that she found the story again and asked Andrea if she wanted to draw pictures for the story. Andrea loved the idea and they worked together to produce a story that they are both very proud of.

It is a story which holds a special place in their hearts and they are happy and excited to share it with you all.

Special thanks go to Alfie and Hilda Ong, to Kamal and to Joshua.

Printed in Great Britain
by Amazon